NAME YOUR EMOTIONS

SOMETIMES I FEEL EMBARRASSED

by Jaclyn Jaycox

PEBBLE
a capstone imprint

Pebble Emerge is published by Pebble, an imprint of Capstone.
1710 Roe Crest Drive
North Mankato, Minnesota 56003
www.capstonepub.com

Library of Congress Cataloging-in-Publication Data is available on the
Library of Congress website.
ISBN 978-1-9771-2466-1 (library binding)
ISBN 978-1-9771-2642-9 (paperback)
ISBN 978-1-9771-2509-5 (eBook PDF)

Summary: What does it mean to be embarrassed? Learn what
embarrassment feels like and what may trigger this emotion. Children
will explore different ways to deal with their feelings and turn bad
feelings into good ones. A mindfulness activity will give kids the chance
to practice managing their emotion.

Image Credits
Capstone Studio: Karon Dubke, 21; Shutterstock: Africa Studio, 15,
Anatoliy Karlyuk, Cover, Color Symphony, Design Element, Halfpoint,
19, Jane September, 6, Kisialiou Yury, 14, Leszek Glasner, 18, Monkey
Business Images, 5, 13, Nikolai Kazakov, 7, Syda Productions, 17, Veja,
11, wavebreakmedia, 9

Editorial Credits
Designer: Kay Fraser; Media Researcher: Tracy Cummins; Production
Specialist: Katy LaVigne

TABLE OF CONTENTS

Words in **bold** are in the glossary.

WHAT IS EMBARRASSMENT?

Imagine eating lunch with your friends. You are all talking and laughing. Suddenly, you let out a big burp. Your friends start to giggle. You might feel a little embarrassed.

Embarrassment is an **emotion**, or feeling. Some emotions can make us feel good. Being embarrassed can make us feel bad.

WHAT DOES IT FEEL LIKE TO BE EMBARRASSED?

Try to think of a time you were embarrassed. Maybe you spilled food on yourself. Maybe you tripped and fell. How did you feel?

When you are embarrassed, your cheeks turn red. Your heart races. You might start to sweat. You feel like you want to run and hide. You might even feel like crying.

USING YOUR SENSES

Everyone has five **senses**. People can touch, taste, and smell things. They also see and hear things. Your senses send messages to your brain. That's where feelings start. Hearing someone laugh at you can make you feel embarrassed.

TALKING ABOUT YOUR FEELINGS

It's not fun to feel embarrassed. But it's important to talk about your feelings. Tell a family member or friend if you are embarrassed. Talk to them about why you feel this way. They can help you feel better. Chances are they have felt the same way.

UNDERSTANDING EMBARRASSMENT

As you grow up, you spend more time with friends. You care what they think of you. So when you make a mistake, you might feel embarrassed. But everyone makes mistakes! You can learn from mistakes.

Your teacher may call on you in class. If you answer wrong, you may feel embarrassed. Even though it feels bad, it's a healthy emotion.

It means you care about making mistakes. You can turn that feeling into something **positive**. It might make you want to study more.

HANDLING YOUR FEELINGS

It's important to know how to handle your feelings. When you feel embarrassed, talk to a parent or friend. Ask them to tell you about a time they felt the same way.

Be kind to yourself. Sometimes you will make mistakes. And they aren't always your fault. Forgive yourself.

Do something to take your mind off of what embarrassed you. Play outside with friends. Do an art project with your little brother. Watch a funny movie.

You can help others who feel embarrassed too. Don't laugh when someone makes a mistake. Be a good listener to a friend who was embarrassed.

MINDFULNESS ACTIVITY

It can be hard to take your mind off of an embarrassing moment. Try to relax with a buddy and turn your focus on yourself.

What You Do:

1. Grab your favorite stuffed animal.

2. Lay on the floor and rest your buddy on your stomach.

3. Take deep breaths. Watch your buddy go up and down as you breathe in and out.

4. Think of each breath in as a bubble. Put any bad thoughts into the bubble. When you breathe out, blow that bubble away!

GLOSSARY

emotion (i-MOH-shuhn)—a strong feeling; people have and show emotions such as happiness, sadness, fear, anger, and jealousy

positive (PAH-zi-tiv)—helpful or upbeat

sense (SENSS)—a way of knowing about your surroundings; hearing, smelling, touching, tasting, and sight are the five senses

READ MORE

Haley, Charly. *Embarrassed*. Mankato, MN: Child's World, 2019.

Kreul, Holde. *My Feelings and Me*. New York: Skyhorse Publishing, 2018.

INTERNET SITES

Emotions Coloring Pages
coloring.ws/emotion.htm

PBS Kids – Draw Your Feelings
pbskids.org/arthur/health/resilience/draw-your-feelings.html

INDEX